W9-AMT-532

37516001950008

Let's Go
CAMPING

Suzanne Slade

PowerKiDS press.

New York

To Jim, Ellen, Patrick, and Michael Hughes, happy campers in all kinds of weather

Published in 2007 by The Rosen Publishing Group, Inc.
29 East 21st Street, New York, NY 10010

First Edition

Editor: Amelie von Zumbusch
Book Design: Dean Galiano and Erica Clendening
Layout Design: Julio Gil

Photo Credits: Cover, p. 10 © Getty Images; pp. 4, 9, 12, 15, 18, 24, 25, 28 © www.shutterstock.com; p. 6 NPS Photo by Jim Peaco; p. 7 © www.istockphoto.com/Jeffrey Logan; p. 8 NPS Photo by Ed Austin & Herb Jones; p. 14 NPS Photo by J. Schmidt; p. 16 U.S. Fish and Wildlife Service. Photo by Phil Knudsen; p. 20 © www.istockphoto.com/phdpsx; p. 21 © www.istockphoto.com/flisk; p. 22 © Ariel Skelley/Corbis; p. 26 NPS Photo by Harlan Kredit; p. 27 © www.istockphoto.com/Paige Falk; p. 29 Courtesy of Suzanne Slade.

Library of Congress Cataloging-in-Publication Data

Slade, Suzanne.
   Let's go camping / Suzanne Slade. — 1st ed.
      p. cm. — (Adventures outdoors)
   Includes index.
   ISBN-13: 978-1-4042-3650-9 (library binding)
   ISBN-10: 1-4042-3650-3 (library binding)
   1. Camping—Juvenile literature. I. Title.
   GV191.7.S58 2007
   796.54—dc22

                                    2006019565

Manufactured in the United States of America

Contents

Camping   5

Planning Your Camping Trip   6

Choosing a Campsite   8

Camping Gear   11

Pitching a Tent   13

Camping in All Kinds of Weather   17

Campfire Cooking   19

Around the Campfire   22

Camp Critters   23

Camping and Nature   26

Let's Go Camping!   28

Safety Tips   30

Glossary   31

Index   32

Web Sites   32

Camping

You'll never run out of interesting things to do on a camping trip. Many campers enjoy exploring nature. You can discover different kinds of animals and see how they live in the wild. You might also hike through the forest or swim in a nearby lake.

When the Sun sets, you can watch for bats taking flight. Listen for hooting owls or howling coyotes. Camping takes you away from city lights, so you can see hundreds of twinkling stars. Search the sky for **constellations** or look for the bright **North Star**. You will enjoy the excitement and challenges of setting up a tent, cooking over a fire, and living outside when you go camping.

DID YOU KNOW?

Why not try out camping for a night by setting up a tent at home? It's fun to sleep under the stars in your own backyard!

You can get to know the sounds, sights, and smells of the world at night when you go camping.

Planning Your Camping Trip

To have a successful camping trip, you should plan ahead so you are prepared to live away from home. You can go camping for several weeks or plan a short overnight trip. Most campers stay in a tent or a **recreational vehicle**, which is commonly called an RV. Many state and national parks have **campgrounds**. These campgrounds usually have lakes for swimming and fishing, hiking trails, and bathrooms. Choose a

People can park their RVs at the Fishing Bridge RV Park at Yellowstone National Park, in Wyoming.

Washington State's Olympic National Park offers campsites with beautiful views.

camping location that offers the types of activities your family enjoys.

One of the best things about camping is that you leave your familiar surroundings and try new things. Instead of staring at a TV, you can watch a spider spin a web or a bird feed its babies.

Choosing a Campsite

Parks have a certain number of **campsites**. During the summer months, campsites at popular campgrounds often fill up quickly. You should reserve your campsite before you leave home. The cost for a campsite varies depending on the **facilities** it provides.

Some campsites were created for people who prefer camping without the comforts of home. These

Many parks have picnic areas with tables and benches, like this one.

Some parks have water pumps where you can get water to drink or to wash your dishes.

sites do not have showers, toilets, or running water. People who camp in an RV often want a campsite that provides electricity. Tent campers may want bathrooms and a store nearby. Whichever type of site you choose, make sure you set up camp on dry ground. Stay away from beehives or large anthills. They don't make good camping neighbors.

Camping Gear

You need to bring the proper gear to stay safe and comfortable while camping. Check the weather report before leaving home, so you will know the right type of clothing to pack. It is helpful to dress in layers. If the day gets warmer, you can quickly adapt to the weather. You should have boots or sneakers to protect your feet from rocks, insects, and sharp plants. Bring a backpack to carry necessary things, such as food, water, sunblock, and bug spray, when you leave the campsite.

DID YOU KNOW?
Don't forget to take a first aid kit. You want to be prepared if an accident happens.

For a good night of sleep, don't forget a sleeping bag and your favorite pillow. Some campers even put a foam pad under their sleeping bag so they won't feel the hard ground under their bed.

While many people like to sleep in tents or RVs, some campers prefer sleeping under the stars.

Pitching a Tent

A tent is a camper's home away from home. Some people like small, simple tents, while others prefer fancy tents with lots of features. Although different campers choose different tents, most agree that the first thing you should do at your campsite is to put up your tent.

Tents vary in size from small, one-person tents to large tents that hold six to eight people. There are three basic kinds of tents. An A-frame tent has two sloping sides that meet at a pointed top. A dome tent has a rounded shape. The third type of tent is a

DID YOU KNOW?

Another type of tent that is often used by hikers is called a hoop tent. This small tent is held up by round, flexible poles called hoops. A hoop tent is light and easy to carry.

These backpackers are setting up their tent. Most tents fold up easily so that backpackers can carry them.

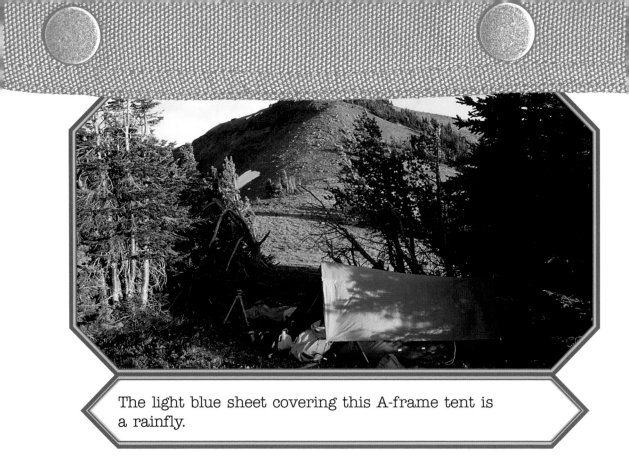

The light blue sheet covering this A-frame tent is a rainfly.

cabin tent. It looks like a house with four straight walls and an angled roof. Some large tents have cloth walls that divide the tent into several rooms.

A tent with windows is great for hot weather. Tent windows have cloth screens, which let air flow through but keep bugs out. You can put a **rainfly** over some tents to protect them from the rain and hot sun. A rainfly fits over a tent like a big blanket. Some tents have a window in the roof, called a skylight. This lets light in and allows you to see the stars at night.

Before setting up your tent, clear the area of rocks and sticks. Most tents are easy to pitch, or set up. Thin, **flexible** poles hold a tent up. The poles slide through loops on the outside of the tent. You can fasten your tent to the ground with stakes.

This girl is fastening the poles to her tent. Tent poles are often made of metal or wood.

Camping in All Kinds of Weather

Everyone hopes for sunny days on a camping trip, but campers must be prepared for all kinds of weather. Be sure to pitch your tent on high ground so water will run away from your tent if it rains. Pack an umbrella so you can stay dry if you go outside. You can add more layers of clothing if the weather turns cold. If winds become strong, place large rocks over the tent stakes to keep your tent from blowing away.

DID YOU KNOW?
Your body loses most of its heat through your head. Wear a hat in cold weather to stay warm.

Remember to pack some books and games. While listening to the sound of raindrops on your tent, you can enjoy playing cards or a board game. You could also have family reading time. Everyone can take turns reading a chapter out loud.

Some people camp in cold, snowy weather. They need sturdy tents, warm clothes, and thick sleeping bags.

Campfire Cooking

One of your best camping memories may be cooking over an open fire. Eating a delicious meal that you cooked can be very rewarding. The challenge of campfire cooking is a great camping experience.

Your first task when cooking a meal is to make a campfire. Start by putting crushed paper in the center of your campsite's fire pit. Then place small, dry sticks around the paper in an upright position. Ask an adult to light the paper. After the sticks begin to burn, add larger logs around the fire. Always keep a bucket of water nearby in case you need to put out your fire.

There are many simple dishes you can make over a campfire. It's easy to cook hot dogs on a

A ring of stones around a campfire will keep the wood in place, block the wind, and hold in the fire's heat.

You can put a kettle over your campfire to boil water for tea or hot chocolate.

stick. Heat some baked beans in a pot, and then you have a tasty dinner.

Another favorite camping meal is cooked in a **foil** pouch. Place loose hamburger meat and thinly cut pieces of carrots and potatoes on a piece of foil. Then fold the foil to seal the sides and top. Place the pouch on hot coals or on a metal **grate** over your fire. The food is ready when the hamburger is brown and the vegetables are soft.

If you have a frying pan, you can fry hamburgers and potatoes for a quick lunch. A popular camping dessert is s'mores. You can create this sweet treat by putting roasted **marshmallows** and pieces of chocolate between **graham crackers**.

Kebabs are a great campfire food. Stick vegetables and meat on long, thin sticks called skewers to make kebabs.

Around the Campfire

It feels great to sit around a campfire when a cool evening breeze blows in. This is a special time when everyone can share the exciting details of the day. You can tell about an adventure you had or an interesting animal you saw. Some campers like to tell stories. What is your favorite bedtime tale? Do you have a scary ghost story you like to tell?

Many people enjoy singing songs around the campfire. Some people even bring along a guitar or **harmonica** to play. As you tap your feet to the music, watch for shooting stars. Enjoy your friends, family, and the warmth of a glowing fire as you relax after a day filled with fun camping activities.

Campfires are a perfect place to roast marshmallows and laugh with your friends.

Camp Critters

Animals are very interesting to observe, but you need to be careful around animals in the wild. Never approach or corner an animal. It might get scared and attack you. When walking through the woods, watch the trail for snakes. Snakes are often slow to move away when people walk near. Some snakes will bite people.

Grizzly bears are rare. You might see one while camping, though, since most live in national parks.

Raccoons are smart and very good with their hands. They are good at figuring out how to steal food.

Animals such as raccoons and bears have a keen sense of smell. Don't leave food lying out. Store all food outside your tent. Animals can rip a hole in a tent if they smell food inside. Some campers put their food in a large bag. They hang the bag from a tree where animals can't reach it. You can also keep food in your car.

25

Camping and Nature

Campers love nature. They like to be outside and discover new things in the living world. Most campgrounds are wonderful places to visit because campers take good care of them. A common rule of camping is leave no trace. This means take everything out of the campground that you brought in. Don't leave any trash or food scraps behind.

There are many beautiful places to camp in national parks. This tent is in Yellowstone National Park.

These campers have pitched their tent on Arizona's Horseshoe Mesa. It is near the Grand Canyon.

People who go camping also respect plants. They know it is best not to pick flowers or berries. They leave them for other people to see or animals to eat. Campers do not break off living branches to build a fire. If you take care of nature, then people will be able to enjoy the beauty of campgrounds for many years.

Let's Go Camping!

Camping is a great way to try new outdoor activities. Many campgrounds have special areas where you can learn to rock climb, swim, sail, and canoe. Some have instructors who teach campers how to ride a horse or shoot arrows with a bow. Other campgrounds offer art classes, such as painting, drawing, or leather-working classes. There are also plenty of activities to do on your

This boy is rock climbing in Billings, Montana. Rock climbing takes lots of strength and training.

If you want to take your dog camping, call the campground first to find out if pets are allowed.

own. You can hike with a friend or drop your fishing line in a lake.

When you go camping, there's always something new to see and do. Your days are filled with adventure and fun. Campers wake to the smell of fresh air and fall asleep to the sound of singing crickets.

Let's go camping!

Safety Tips

- Protect yourself from getting burned by the sun. Wear a hat and plenty of sunblock.

- Don't hike by yourself. Always go with a friend.

- Put out your fire completely before leaving your campsite.

- If you don't know how to swim, wear a life jacket anytime you are around water.

- Don't eat berries you find in the woods. They may make you sick.

- On hot days make sure to drink lots of water.

- Use a map or mark your trail so you don't get lost in the woods.

- Follow the park safety rules and obey any warning signs you see in the park.

- If you leave your campsite to do an activity, be sure to come back before it gets dark.

- Don't drink water from a river or lake.

Glossary

campgrounds (KAMP-growndz) Areas reserved for camping.

campsites (KAMP-syts) Places where people set up camp.

constellations (kon-stuh-LAY-shunz) Groups of stars.

facilities (fuh-SIH-luh-teez) Things built for a certain function.

flexible (FLEK-sih-bul) Being able to move and bend in many ways.

foil (FOYL) A thin, bendable sheet of metal.

graham crackers (GRAM KRA-kerz) Sweet crackers made from whole wheat flour.

grate (GRAYT) A frame of metal bars.

harmonica (hahr-MAH-nih-kuh) A small musical instrument with slots to blow into.

marshmallows (MAHRSH-meh-lohz) Spongelike foods made from whipped sugar.

North Star (NORTH STAHR) One of the brightest stars.

rainfly (RAYN-fly) A waterproof sheet that covers a tent.

recreational vehicle (reh-kree-AY-shnul VEE-uh-kul) A van you can both drive and live in.

Index

A
activities, 7, 23, 28
animals, 5, 24–25, 27

B
bathrooms, 6, 9
boots, 11

C
campgrounds, 6, 8, 26–28
clothing, 11, 17
constellations, 5

F
facilities, 8

forest, 5

G
grate, 20

H
harmonica, 23

L
lake(s), 5–6, 29

M
meal(s), 19–20

N
national parks, 6
North Star, 5

P
poles, 15

R
rainfly, 14
recreational vehicle (RV), 6, 9

S
s'mores, 21
sneakers, 11

T
tent(s), 5–6, 13–15, 17, 25
trail(s), 6, 24

Web Sites

Due to the changing nature of Internet links, PowerKids Press has developed an online list of Web sites related to this book. This site is updated regularly. Please use this link to access the list: www.powerkidslinks.com/adout/camping/